Dedication

I dedicate this book to my grandmother, Dorothy Grace. I thank you for always showing me the love of Christ and encouraging me to be the woman God intended me to be. You are my inspiration and my mentor. I love you Maw Maw!

Scripture

I praise you because you made me in an amazing and wonderful way.
What you have done is wonderful. I know this very well. Psalms 139:14 ICB

Bailey saw Mr. Robin
perched on a limb,
So Bailey went over
to talk to him.

Mr. Robin said, "Hi there, how do you do?"

Bailey smiled and said, "I am good, how are you?"

Mr. Robin said, "I'm fine,
just perched here to see
All the things going on
around me."

Bailey thought for a minute
and he said with a frown,
"But I cannot see those
things here from the
ground."

Bailey thought about Mr. Robin flying high in the sky And he began to wish that he, too, could fly.

Bailey said to Mr. Robin, "oh, how can it be
That you are you and I am stuck being me?"

Mr. Robin spoke up and said,
"Now don't you fret,
Being yourself you
should never regret.

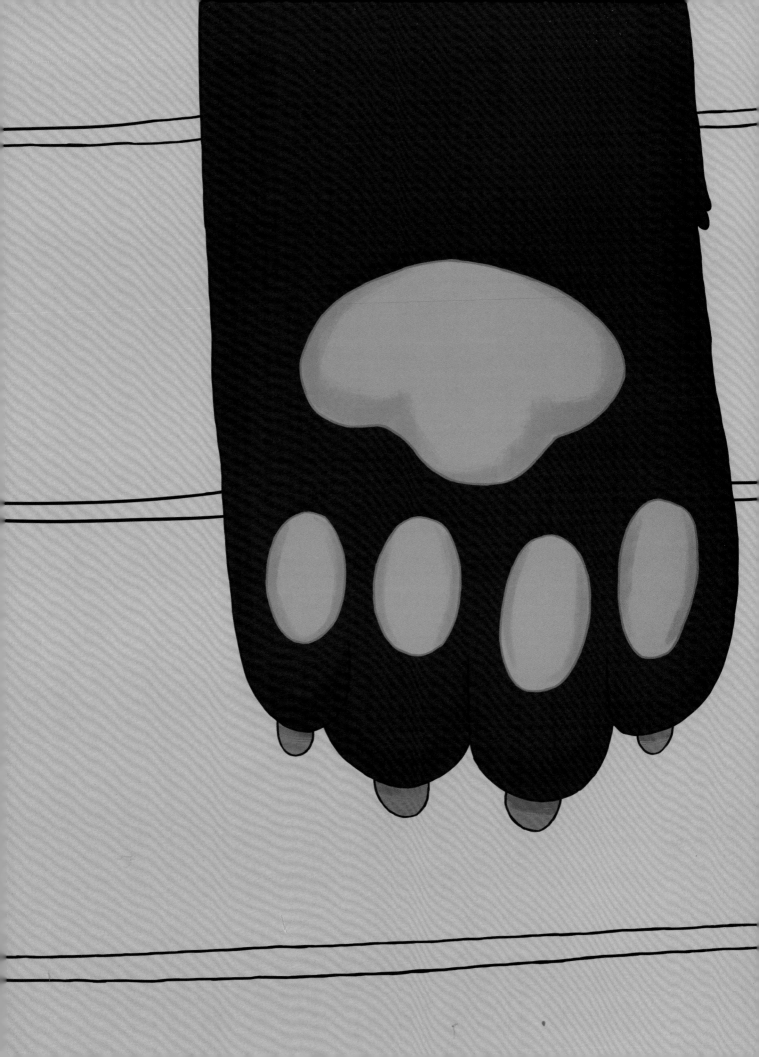

For each of us is special in
our very own way
And we should thank God for
that each and every day

For He made all of us as special
as special can be,
So I should not want to be you -
nor should you want to be me.

It is true I can spread my
wings and fly high in the sky
And I can see the beauty of
everything from way up high

But you are able to do
things that I cannot do
And there are times I admit
that I would like to be you.

You can play chase with your
friends all through the fields
and help sniff out things that
might have been concealed.

You can work with search and
rescue saving people's lives,
You are man's best friend -
which no one can deny."

Bailey thought for a minute and realized his friend was right. "Oh, thank you, Mr. Robin for showing me the light.

I realize now that God made
me how he wants me to be
And I am really very happy
just being me."

AUTHOR BIOGRAPHY

Debbie Barber is a writer of children's books and poetry. She loves to write books to enrich her reader's lives. Her Yorkshire Terrier, Bailey, is the main character in her line of Bailey Books.

Debbie lives in Greenville, North Carolina, with Bailey and her husband, Jimmy. She is a member of the Just Write writing group. When Debbie is not working or writing, you can find her lending a helping hand to those less fortunate in her community.